Pick a Powerpuff Path

hide-and-go mojo

by Peter David

Scholastic Inc.
New York • Toronto • London • Auckland • Sydney
Mexico City • New Delhi • Hong Kong • Buenos Aires

ISBN 0-439-33249-4

Cover and interior illustrations by Bill Alger

Designed by Mark Neston

12 11 10 9 8 7 6 5 4 3 2 1   2 3 4 5 6 7/0

Printed in the U.S.A.

First Scholastic printing, March 2002

Read This First!

Sugar...Spice...and Everything Nice...

These were the ingredients chosen to create the perfect little girls. But Professor Utonium accidentally added an extra ingredient to the concoction—Chemical X!

And thus, The Powerpuff Girls were born! Using their ultra superpowers, Blossom, Bubbles, and Buttercup have dedicated their lives to fighting crime and the forces of evil!

One of those forces of evil is Mojo Jojo. Once the Professor's clumsy monkey lab assistant, he's now a brainy supervillain utterly devoted to destroying those pesky Powerpuff Girls!

Here's your chance to be on the side of the bad guys, as Mojo chases after the Girls in his brand-new robot, the Mojobot! The story will have different outcomes depending on the choices you make. Decide on the direction of the story when given a choice, and see what happens next. When you're done, you can start over and make other choices and read a completely new story.

Of course, The Powerpuff Girls have never lost... before. Will they be utterly defeated this time by the sinister monkey mastermind? The choices you make will decide that!

The city of Townsville! A place that's happy and protected, and the home of the toughest kindergartners around: The Powerpuff Girls!

Even though most people in Townsville loved and adored The Powerpuff Girls, there was one person who wasn't crazy about them at all! He wasn't really a "person," actually. No, he was a monkey! A monkey with a superbrain. He lived in Townsville Observatory, set on the top of a volcano in the middle of Townsville Park, and his name was Mojo Jojo.

Mojo used to be a lab monkey working for Professor Utonium, creator of The Powerpuff Girls. But once the Professor created the Girls, he ignored Mojo Jojo. So Mojo was tremendously jealous of the threesome and loved to come up with plans that he hoped would put an end to their happiness once and for all! And one day, he was putting the finishing touches on what he thought would be the greatest device ever made to destroy The Powerpuff Girls!

"Haaa-ha-ha! This is the greatest device ever made to destroy The Powerpuff Girls!" Mojo cackled. He ran all over his secret lair, grabbing up one tool after another, going back and forth to his new device. "Yes, I...Mojo Jojo, supergenius evil monkey, will finally triumph!! And soon, The Powerpuff Girls will be in my power! It will be my power they are in!"

And Mojo had good reason to gloat! For he had just developed his newest giant robot. His new Mojobot was 10 feet high. Mojo usually preferred to build 50-foot-tall robots, because they looked so scary. But this smaller-than-usual giant robot would let Mojo operate indoors, too—as long as the building had high ceilings. When he rode around inside the top of the Mojobot, Mojo could control every move it made! Through the clear dome on top, Mojo could see all around, and the Mojobot had a variety of gadgets that let him see and hear things from a mile away.

"And it comes fully loaded!" Mojo exclaimed to himself. "It has a portable laser, super-strength, giant sticky nets, the power of flight, and an espresso machine just in case I need a little something to keep me awake!"

There was just one thing that made Mojo a little nervous. His Mojobot was powered by a mineral called Punkium, which came in fist-sized chunks and was very rare. "Curse my luck!" muttered Mojo when he was doing the final checks. "I've only got enough Punkium to last for one hour. If I want to destroy The Powerpuff Girls, I am really going to have to hurry!"

Ding dong!

Professor Utonium opened the door of his house, where he and The Powerpuff Girls lived, and saw a very strange-looking, short, furry man standing there. There was also a giant robot next to him. The man was wearing a gray suit and glasses. *Any dope would have known that it is I, Mojo Jojo, in a cunning disguise,* thought Mojo, *but the Professor isn't just any dope! He is an extremely trusting dope!*

"Hello!" said the disguised monkey genius. "I am Ned McMann! I'm from the Publishers Steering House, and I'm here to tell you that The Powerpuff Girls have won a contest. This is their prize!" He pointed at the giant robot. "Would you care to send them out so I can...GIVE IT TO THEM!"

His disguise worked perfectly, fooling the Professor. But it wasn't going to be as easy as all that, because the Professor said, "Bad timing, I'm afraid. The Girls picked today to have a daylong game of hide-and-seek. They're out hiding somewhere in Townsville. I have no idea where they might be."

"No idea at all?" the masked monkey master-mind asked. "None? At all? No ideas? No clues, notions, concepts, best guesses—"

"Well," said the Professor thoughtfully, "I do seem to recall something about a used toy sale at a vacant house across the street from Pokey Oaks Kindergarten. Some of the Girls' classmates and their teacher, Ms. Keane, were involved with it. I think the Girls were going to stop by there first." The Professor laughed. "But they've probably left there by now and are off hiding at some familiar place, like the Mayor's office or the bank—heaven knows they've stopped it from being robbed enough times!"

"Yes, well, thanks for nothing," Mojo muttered in annoyance, and the Professor closed the door. *Where would be the best place to start looking for the Girls?* wondered Mojo.

If Mojo Jojo decides to look for the Girls at the used toy sale at the vacant house across from Pokey Oaks Kindergarten, turn to page 26.

If Mojo Jojo decides to look for the Girls at the Mayor's office, turn to page 42.

If Mojo Jojo decides to look for the Girls at the bank, turn to page 52.

"The last thing I need is damage to my reputation," said Mojo to himself. "I am, after all, Mojo Jojo, a super-genius evil monkey. I don't want people getting the wrong idea, thinking I'm going soft, when that is the total opposite way I'm going. In fact, the best thing I could do to make sure that everyone knows I am still evil is to rob the bank myself!"

Mojo slammed the Mojobot's control levers forward, and the robot moved toward the locked vault. It would be no problem at all for Mojo to rip the door clean off with the power in his Mojobot arms!

But before he could do so, there was a popping noise behind him, and a high, silky voice said, "Well, well...what have we here?" Mojo looked down from the control dome of the Mojobot and saw...Him! Him, the ultimate evil one...and he did not look happy with Mojo at all!

"Villains making life difficult for other villains?" Him said, shaking his head, sounding very disappointed. "That's sooooo impolite, Mojo! I'm afraid I just can't stand by and see that happen."

Mojo Jojo didn't like the sound of this. Him was all-powerful. On the other hand, Mojo's Mojobot was no slouch, either.

If Mojo decides to stay and try to slug it out with Him, turn to page 16.

If Mojo decides that getting out of there would be a good idea, turn to page 21.

8

"How dare this stupid, firecracker-throwing monster wreck Townsville on this day!" said Mojo. "This should be my day to wreck Townsville! In fact, when I get done...every day will be Mojo Wrecks Townsville Day!"

Mojo activated his weapons and the Mojobot charged forward. The squid saw him coming, but thought he was looking at an oversized toy soldier. Picking the Mojobot up in his many arms, the squid grinned and waved the Mojobot around as if it were an oversized rattle.

"All right! That's enough of that!" said Mojo. "In fact...that's more than enough! It's sufficient!" Mojo fired up his jets and headed skyward, the squid still holding on! Mojo spun in the air like a top. For several minutes Mojo kept it up, and the squid got dizzier and dizzier. Eventually, the monster couldn't hold on anymore and went flying halfway back to Monster Isle! Mojo had defeated the firecracker-throwing squid!

But as Mojo landed on the ground, his Punkium used up, he was horrified to see that the people of Townsville were running up to him...and thanking him! *They think I saved them because...I am a nice guy!* Mojo thought, utterly disgusted. *Ughhh!* And he didn't have enough power to fly away, so he had to stand there and take all the praise and love Townsville was heaping on him! "Gahhh! I'd take power-punches over this any day!" groaned Mojo to himself.

Continue on page 64.

Princess's father was the richest man in Townsville. Mojo couldn't pass up the shot at whatever reward Mr. Morbucks might hand him for saving his little girl.

Mojo barreled after Blossom, determined to catch up with her. Even carrying Princess, Blossom still moved like lightning, but Mojo gunned the Mojobot's jet boots, picked up speed, and flew faster and faster....

Zooming along at top speed, Mojo Jojo managed to sneak up behind Blossom and her prisoner. With pinpoint aim, Mojo blasted Blossom with his laser set at full power! It was a direct hit!

"Ha! That knocked the power out of you, Powerpuff Girl!" crowed Mojo as he watched Blossom tumbling to the ground. "Now you're just...a puff! And I, Mojo, have...uh-oh."

Mojo saw that Princess was tumbling toward the ground, too, yelling her head off the whole way down! *Her daddy won't pay much of a reward if his little girl ends up flatter than a pancake!* thought Mojo.

"Stop that irritating screaming, you annoying brat! It's hurting my sensitive ears, which are being irritated by all that annoying screaming!" complained Mojo as he caught Princess in one huge metal hand of his Mojobot.

Mojo then flew to the ground to check out Blossom. She wasn't hurt, of course: The Powerpuff Girls were too tough for that. But she'd been knocked out for a few minutes.

"Ha! Sugar and spice and everything nice! And seeing you helpless is nice indeed!" laughed Mojo. *And I deserve to laugh,* thought Mojo, *because I, Mojo Jojo, have just defeated one of The Powerpuff Girls!*

"Well done, Mojo!" said the pleased Princess. "Come with me to my house, and my daddy will give you a reward!" Mojo could definitely use the money—evil plots were usually terribly expensive to carry out. However, Mojo still had today's evil plot to finish; he had already managed to defeat one of The Powerpuff Girls...and if he hurried, he might be able to defeat the other two, too!

If Mojo Jojo goes with Princess to collect the reward from Mr. Morbucks, turn to page 36.

If Mojo tries chasing down the other two Powerpuff Girls to defeat them first, turn to page 39.

Mojo Jojo certainly had no intention of picking up the leftovers of the Gangreen Gang! He, Mojo Jojo, was the one with the robot. Let the Gangreen Gang get their own bank...maybe one in some other city! "But this city, and this bank, belong to... Mohhhhhjo Jojo!" he announced.

Mojo Jojo stomped into the bank, blaring through his loudspeaker, "All right, you interfering blunderers! This is Mojo Jojo, and I want you out! Gone! Departed! Not in! But out! Out! Out!"

The Gangreen Gang thought they could stop Mojo! "Time for some monkeyshines, boys!" shouted their leader, Ace. They came at Mojo with everything they had...which would have been great, if they'd actually had anything. Unfortunately for them, the Gangreen Gang didn't have any weapons. Big Billy was in charge of them today, and he'd forgotten to bring any!

The Gangreen Gang punched the Mojobot, but that didn't do anything except hurt their hands. In the meantime, Mojo picked up fallen pieces of rubble with his Mojobot's hands and started throwing them at the Gang. The Gang members didn't know which way to run first, so they ran in all directions at once and crashed into one another.

The Gangreen Gang soon realized that they didn't stand a chance against Mojo! "This isn't over yet, monkey boy!" they shouted, even as they backpedaled and ran out into the streets. Within seconds, the Gang had made themselves scarce.

And then, to Mojo's horror and amazement, reporters, customers, and bank employees ran up to him and thanked him! *They...they think I'm a*

hero for chasing off the Gangreen Gang! he
thought in disgust. *They don't realize that I did it
because the Gangreen Gang was horning in on* my
*bank. They think I've decided to turn good or
something! Well, this is unacceptable! Something
has to be done!*

Mojo considered just cleaning out the bank himself then and there...but his Punkium might start
to run down. And he still needed to find those
accursed Powerpuff Girls!

If Mojo decides to stay and clean out the bank
himself, turn to page 8.

If Mojo decides to get the heck out of there and
continue his time-imperative search for The Powerpuff
Girls, turn to page 18.

13

"Okay, Mojo, let's see what you've got!" shouted Blossom.

And Mojo was more than ready to show her! He fired one of his super-sticky nets at Blossom, and it completely surrounded her. She tried to shake it off, but she couldn't! "It'll take more than that, Mojo Jojo!" Blossom said, and she fired twin eye blasts at him. It staggered him and knocked the Mojobot flat, but it didn't stop Mojo!

"Oh, I've got more than that," Mojo told her as Blossom came at him, ready with a power punch. The floor was shaking and the air was filled with noise as they went at each other. *Pow! Zak! Blammo!*

Through the dust in the air Mojo could see Sedusa, who looked very angry at being shoved aside. She was shouting, "You won't get away with this! I was willing to fight Blossom with you, but you just want to steal all of the glory yourself! You'll be sorry!"

But Mojo didn't listen; the super-genius evil monkey was far too busy to pay attention. Neither Mojo nor Blossom was backing down. The whole place was starting to shake from the strain of their battle, and Mojo was worried that his Punkium would run down...but then Blossom looked like she was starting to wear out....

And then, *whammo!* Blossom went flying, knocking the roof of Townsville City Hall clean off as she crashed through it. "Haaa-ha-ha-ha! I have done it! I have defeated one of The Powerpuff Girls!" Mojo said. "Blossom did not win! I won! Because I am the winner, and she is the loser!"

But Mojo's triumph didn't last. As Mojo stomped out of the Mayor's office, he saw a crowd of angry-looking supervillains gathering outside.

Continue on page 30.

Mojo took a deep gulp and tried to get himself ready for battle. "Take your best shot!" Mojo declared to Him.

"Meeee?" Him said, sounding surprised Mojo would even mention it. "No, no...I would never get my claws dirty fighting you myself."

Mojo let out a sigh of relief. Him had just been bluffing!

Then Him said, "However, I did take the liberty of letting an assortment of your fellow bad guys out of jail and telling them all that you'd turned against the cause of evil. They didn't take it well...no, not at all. Well...ta ta!"

Mojo looked around in alarm as every villain he'd ever known, met, or had an occasional brunch with charged toward him from all directions. Him disappeared...but his vanishing was the least of Mojo's problems!

Continue on page 30.

Mojo grabbed a tool kit and started trying to rewire the Mojobot's busted insides. But he was having no luck at all. Still...maybe if he crossed those two wires, the blue and the red wire, it might reactivate the Mojobot....

Zzzzzt! Zaaaaak!

Well, the good news was Mojo had managed to get the FM stations up and running on his internal radio. That, and his searchlight was working. The bad news was nothing *else* was working...and now water was pouring in from everywhere. It looked like this was the end!

Continue on page 19.

If there was one thing that he, Mojo, had—aside from a terrific robot, a super-genius mind, and a really great classical music CD collection—it was his priorities in place! Nothing was going to be served standing around here when there were Powerpuff Girls to destroy.

Without another word, he flew off, up into the sky, looking around and trying to find his targets, the source of his biggest irritation. "Where are they hiding?" he growled. "For that matter, *why* are they hiding? Don't they know that I, Mojo Jojo, am taking time out from my busy day to hunt them down and destroy them? The least they could do is be considerate of my timetable!"

But then he saw a small red-haired female form jetting across the sky! *It could be Blossom!* Mojo thought excitedly. Immediately Mojo took off in that direction.

Continue on page 44.

18

Suddenly, there was a break in the water above Mojo Jojo! It was...Buttercup! And obviously, she was trying to find him! She hadn't spotted him, though, because he was on the bottom of the lake. However, since he'd gotten his searchlight working, he could turn it on and shine it so that she could spot him. It would be humiliating to be rescued by a Powerpuff Girl! But if he didn't get her attention fast, he was doomed!

If Mojo swallows his pride and signals Buttercup, turn to page 20.

If Mojo decides not to signal Buttercup, turn to page 60.

Mojo cursed to himself, even as he turned on the Mojobot's searchlight. Sure enough, Buttercup spotted him and zipped right down toward him. Mojo could see that she was really looking forward to rescuing him.

Buttercup tugged on the Mojobot, but it was stuck in the muck at the bottom. "Wonderful! After all that, I'm going to drown anyway!" said Mojo. "Then again, maybe that's better than owing my life to a Powerpuff Girl. The only thing worse than that would be...oh, no!"

Oh, yes, it *was* worse than that! He was going to owe his life to all *three* Powerpuff Girls, because here came Buttercup's sisters, Blossom and Bubbles! With the three of them operating as a team, they were able to haul Mojo out of the lake and to safety on the shore. There, they pulled him out, sputtering and gasping for air.

"Well, Girls, thanks a lot...time to go," Mojo said, but of course the Girls weren't about to let him get away. Instead they dragged him away to jail. Mojo Jojo was left with no pride, no loot, and no Mojobot. What he *did* have, however, was the beginning of a new plan that would defeat The Powerpuff Girls forever! *Curse those Powerpuff Girls!*

Continue on page 61.

"All-powerful" meant "all-powerful," and it meant bad news for Mojo if he stayed around to fight Him. "The last thing I need to do is muck around with that evil super-villain...so that's the last thing I'm going to do!" declared Mojo Jojo. Mojo flew the  Mojobot away from there as fast as he could, leaving Him laughing behind him.

Suddenly, Mojo caught a flash of movement far in the distance. It seemed to be a little red-haired girl, zipping across the sky at high speed. *It's probably that accursed Blossom,* Mojo thought. But at the same time, Mojo heard screaming and shouting from the direction of the Townsville Bridge. Even from this distance, he could see a giant monster destroying the bridge. *Another monster,* Mojo thought. *Once those foolish Girls find out about the monster, they'll cease their ridiculous hide-and-seek game and go after it.* Mojo could wait for the Girls at the bridge, but he'd have to be careful—the monster could decide to go after *him* instead!

If Mojo decides to go after the flying red-haired girl, turn to page 44.

If Mojo decides to go to the bridge, turn to page 40.

Squish squash squish squash.

That was the sound of Mojo Jojo walking home. This had definitely not been his best day. He was soaked through and through, his waterproof watch had stopped working, the outfit he was wearing was dry-clean only, and worst of all, he was going

to smell like wet monkey fur for days.

Mojo got a ride in the back of a pickup truck loaded with chickens being brought from Farmsville into Townsville. "So this is the smell of defeated evil. It smells like chicken," Mojo growled as the truck dropped him off at his secret lab atop the volcano in the middle of town. There he went up to his living room, plucked chicken feathers out of his fur, flopped down into his chair (squishing, naturally), put on some relaxing classical music, and proceeded to plan his next endeavor against those infuriating little brats.

Curse those Powerpuff Girls! Nice music, though, Mojo thought.

Continue on page 61.

Mojo's glee was short-lived, because at that moment, the other two Powerpuff Girls, Bubbles and Blossom (who seemed to have recovered completely from her earlier battle with Mojo), came flying into the room at full speed. They must have figured out Buttercup's plan and come to help her fight Princess! And when Mojo checked the energy level of his Punkium, he saw that it was too low to survive an extended battle with all three! The Girls, however, looked fresh as little daisies! *Can nothing keep them down?* Mojo wondered angrily.

"We found you, Buttercup! And Mojo and Princess, too!" shouted Blossom and Bubbles. Then all three heroines went after Mojo and Princess. Princess let out a yelp and tried to run, but the Girls caught her immediately, and then they converged on Mojo.

Continue on page 61.

Well, what the heck: Mojo had never liked Sedusa all that much, anyway, and a reward was a reward!

"Oh, no you don't, Mojo!" shouted Sedusa, her deadly hair coming at him. But that didn't bother Mojo in the least, because Sedusa was no match for the mighty Mojobot.

"Oh, yes I do, Sedusa!" answered Mojo. His mechanical Mojobot hands moved with lightning speed. He started swinging Sedusa around by the hair, which didn't hurt her any, but sure made her dizzy.

"Knock it off!" Sedusa shouted, but Mojo didn't listen because visions of the reward were dancing in his head.

"What's the matter?" Mojo replied. "Haven't you ever heard of a hair weave?" And within minutes, Sedusa was lying on the floor, unable to move, because Mojo had woven her hair into a form-fitting cocoon. Her arms were pinned to her sides and she couldn't move her legs. She was helpless.

"Hair today, gone tomorrow!" said the Mayor.

"Silence!" Mojo said. "I don't need to stand here and listen to bad jokes. I can go and stand elsewhere for that. You said you had a reward. So fork it over."

"Oh, absolutely, yes," said the Mayor, his voice quivering with emotion. He pulled open a desk drawer and rummaged through it. "The first thing I have to give you is this: one of my most prized possessions—my beloved harmonica!"

Mojo stared in astonishment at his open hand as the Mayor handed him the harmonica. "And the second thing I have for you is my profound thanks," the Mayor added.

"That's...it?" Mojo asked, astonished.

"I don't think you fully appreciate the magnificence of this harmonica," said the Mayor.

Before the monkey supervillain could respond, he heard alarms going off at the bank. It was probably a robbery! And if there was a robbery going on, The Powerpuff Girls might very well show up to stop it. This could be his chance!

Continue on page 52.

Zooming through the air in his Mojobot, Mojo approached the vacant house across from Pokey Oaks Kindergarten. And there he saw that annoying, always-smiling teacher, Ms. Keane, with a bunch of The Powerpuff Girls' little playmates, set up outside the house with tables full of old toys for sale.

But no Powerpuff Girls! No sign of them! Obviously the Professor was right; they'd been there and left. Mojo had used up some of his precious energy source for nothing!

Well, Mojo was going to show everyone who was boss! He made a spectacular landing on top of the vacant house, squashing it flat. Ms. Keane and the children were completely unhurt, but they were clearly astonished by what had happened.

Mojo Jojo clicked on his outside speakers so everyone could hear his voice. "Haaaa-ha-ha-ha!" he shouted, his voice echoing all over the place. "I have destroyed the house where you are selling toys! Now you cannot sell them!"

The children stared up at him, their lower lips quivering, scared by Mojo's booming voice. Then they started crying. "Well, that's certainly annoying," Mojo said to himself. "I don't need to stand around here and listen to them carry on."

Then Mojo heard explosions from the direction of downtown Townsville. He couldn't tell for sure what had caused them, but maybe the Girls would show up downtown to check out the explosions. *On the other hand, considering the racket these children are making,* Mojo thought, *The Powerpuff Girls might hear their noise and show up here instead.*

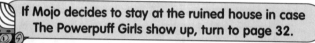

If Mojo decides to stay at the ruined house in case The Powerpuff Girls show up, turn to page 32.

If Mojo decides to check out the explosions, turn to page 38.

A foolish little girl such as Princess has no need for so big and gorgeous a jewel as that! thought Mojo.

Mojo tore across the sky after Princess. Suddenly, Princess saw him coming and figured out what he was after. "Forget it, Mojo!" she shouted, angling away from him even as she fired an electronic shocker gun. It was a nice piece of hardware, and as the electricity slammed through Mojo's Mojobot, it even slowed him down a little. But not enough, not nearly enough!

As Mojo drew closer, Princess held up a shield... with mechanical boxing gloves springing out of it! It pounded on Mojo's armor, even as he blasted away at her shield! The battle carried the two of them across Townsville, firing and pounding on each other, until Mojo had almost closed in on Princess.

Suddenly, Princess dropped the jewel! Mojo zoomed after it, trying to catch it. Straight toward the center of Townsville he went, trying to snag the jewel before it hit the ground and shattered into a million pieces! Closer, closer, and...

"Haaa-ha-ha! I caught it!" said Mojo. "I, Mojo Jojo, have caught it! It is mine...mine!"

Except...

Curses! thought Mojo. *The Powerpuff Girls are here!* Mojo was floating in midair, with the jewel grasped firmly in his Mojobot hand. He would have to get out of the Mojobot in order to install the jewel into the robot's power supply, which was located at the bottom of the robot's left foot. If he left the Mojobot, Mojo would be totally

defenseless against The Powerpuff Girls. But he didn't have enough power left in his Mojobot to take on the Girls! Mojo was in *big* trouble!

Continue on page 54.

Sedusa, the snaky-haired villainess, was at the center of the crowd of annoyed-looking supervillains. "We thought you were one of us, Mojo!" said Sedusa. "We thought we could count on you to back us up! Not back *over* us!"

Mojo started planning his defense, but as he hurriedly checked the display showing the energy reserves of the Mojobot, he discovered that his Punkium had run out!

The villains began coming at him from all sides! With his Punkium run down to nothing, Mojo couldn't put up a defense. Inside of a minute, the bad guys cracked open his control dome and hauled him out.

"All right, now let's discuss this like...*ow! Ooof!* Watch the fur...I just had it groomed! *Akkk!* All

right, that's enough of...*unffff!* Wait! This is
all just a big misunderstand—*ooof! Ouch!* Not the
helmet! Not the helmet! *Ummfffff!*"

It went on like that for a while, and Mojo was
more than ready to call it quits when he heard the
villains crying out, "Oh, no, it's The Powerpuff
Girls!"

The pint-sized heroines had shown up after
all...and now they were going after Mojo's fellow
villains! Mojo Jojo didn't know whether to laugh or
cry...but what he did know was that right now he
could use a very long rest.

Continue on page 61.

"Fine! Cry! Cry your blasted heads off, see if I care," Mojo told the children, figuring that the louder they cried, the sooner The Powerpuff Girls would show up.

And someone did indeed show up...except it wasn't the Girls! Pulling up in a large car was none other than Ms. Sara Bellum, the Mayor's beautiful (and brilliant) assistant. "What happened here, Ms. Keane?" she said, surveying the damage.

"Mojo Jojo just destroyed the vacant house across the street from Pokey Oaks!" said Ms. Keane, and before Mojo could gloat over that, he was horrified to hear, "Wasn't that considerate of him?"

"Whaaaaat?" Mojo said.

"It sure was," said Ms. Bellum. "After all, that's what this toy sale was all about: to raise

money so we could knock down this old house and turn the yard into a new playground for the children. But Mojo Jojo saved us all that money by knocking it down himself! Why, I'll bet the Mayor himself would like to thank him for his help!"

All the children, no longer frightened, were now cheering Mojo Jojo. For an evil supervillain, there was no worse sound in the world. He was not there to make people happy! Part of Mojo wanted to just get out of there...and maybe check out the bank. On the other hand, he had never been thanked by the Mayor before. That might be interesting.

If Mojo decides to look for The Powerpuff Girls at the bank, turn to page 52.

If Mojo decides to head over to the Mayor's office, turn to page 42.

This was perfect! There was Bubbles, her huge eyes shut tight as she counted away, blissfully unaware that what she was really doing was counting down to her own destruction! "Mwwaa-ha-ha-haa!" said Mojo, although he said it very softly so as not to be heard.

As quietly as possible, Mojo flew right up to Bubbles, bringing his onboard speakers as close to her as he could. "Ninety-eight, ninety-nine," she was saying, but Mojo didn't give her the chance to get any further as he blasted his onboard radio at her. It was deafening! Bubbles was sent into a tailspin, clutching her head, unable to concentrate on anything!

Mojo now delivered a series of power plays that sent Bubbles rolling end over end. They battled all the way to the street, and when the dust cleared, there was a Bubbles-sized crater in the ground...and Bubbles was lying in the middle of it. Given how tough The Powerpuff Girls were, she would surely recover soon, but Bubbles seemed to have been knocked out for a few moments.

And for those few moments, Mojo had tri-umphed! He'd defeated one of The Powerpuff Girls!

Continue on page 62.

Mojo figured that a bird in the hand—that is to say, tons of cash—was worth even more than The Powerpuff Girls. After all, Princess's father had more money than all the banks in Townsville combined. Let those Powerpuff Girls play their stupid game of hide-and-seek. He would be rich...really rich!

"After you," Mojo said, figuring it was best if Princess led the way. If nothing else, it was the best way to keep an eye on her.

Off Mojo flew, and within moments he landed outside Princess's house. "I'm pretty sure my daddy is home," Princess told Mojo, "and if he's not, we can wait for him. Let's go to his den." Mojo

didn't like the idea of waiting around, but he didn't have all that much choice at this point. At least the ceilings in Morbucks Mansion were high enough so that he didn't have to leave the Mojobot outside.

Just as they were about to enter the den, Mojo and Princess heard a voice coming from it. It sure didn't sound like Mr. Morbucks....

No! It was...Buttercup's voice, and she was laughing! "This is the perfect plan," Princess and Mojo heard Buttercup saying to herself. "Blossom told me that she doesn't know how Princess managed to attack her and get away. Of course, Blossom's fine now—Princess is no match for one of us. Anyway, sooner or later, Princess'll have to come back home. Good thing that I can fly so much faster than Princess's stupid flying suit! I'll be waiting here for her so I can arrest her...and, in the meantime, I've got the perfect hiding place! 'Cause who'd suspect I'd be hiding in the house of one of our greatest enemies!"

Mojo and Princess looked at each other and grinned. Buttercup might have been expecting Princess...but Princess along with the powerful Mojobot? No way! This was going to be the easiest fight Mojo had ever had.

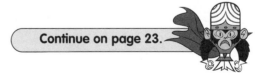

Continue on page 23.

Mojo headed toward the city, wondering what the source of the explosions could possibly be...but when he saw it, he didn't quite believe it.

It was a giant, squidlike monster oozing down the main street of Townsville, throwing off firecrackers in all directions with its many arms. If the squid wasn't stopped, it looked like it would destroy Townsville!

Hey! Destroying Townsville is my job! thought Mojo, seriously upset. *I am supposed to be the most destructive person in Townsville. How can this giant squid think it is allowed to steal my title!* Sure, Mojo had to admit, the squid was doing a great job, but even so...this was supposed to be Mojo's day. He couldn't help but feel just a little jealous.

If Mojo decides to stop the monster, turn to page 9.

If Mojo decides to leave the monster to his explosive business, turn to page 43.

"Nothing must distract me from my first priority, which is the defeat of The Powerpuff Girls!" Mojo said. "Nothing! Not offers of rewards, not money, not prizes, not anything! No...only The Powerpuff Girls are of interest!"

So off Mojo went instead to where he last saw Bubbles.

Continue on page 34.

Mojo hovered by the Townsville Bridge, waiting for the Girls to show up and fiddling with the dials of his Mojobot. He had to come up with a plan of defense quickly, before the monster attacked. Suddenly, the monster yelled and swung a huge, shaggy fist.

Uh-oh, thought Mojo.

Mojo tried to get out of the monster's way, but the monster's fist was just too big! Mojo spiraled end over end, working the instruments as fast as he could to try and regain control over the Mojobot! Within moments, he stabilized the Mojobot. Now, Mojo was mad! No one, not even a huge hairy monster, was allowed to toss Mojo Jojo around like a furry Ping-Pong ball! The Mojobot whipped around, firing at the monster with full laser power! The monster staggered and roared! He swung at Mojo, but this time Mojo darted around the monster's fist. Mojo moved in, blasting away with all of his firepower, but it was no good.

The monster grabbed Mojo in a fist the size of a football field! He was squeezing Mojo as hard as he could! Systems were overloading throughout the Mojobot! Its jets were on full thrust, but Mojo still couldn't shake loose of the monster! Mojo was in big, big trouble....

Suddenly, he heard, "*Oooof! Unhhh! Ooooof!*" It was the monster...and he was caught off guard by Buttercup! Yes, the toughest Powerpuff Girl was going after the monster with everything she had!

"Okay, Steve, this is as far as you get!" she shouted.

Steve? The monster was named Steve? thought Mojo. *What a dull name.*

And suddenly, Mojo was falling! Steve had let go of Mojo to concentrate on Buttercup! But Mojo's jets were out; all of his systems were out, in fact. He couldn't get the Mojobot up and running! Instead, all he could do was drop like a stone!

Mojo hit the water, *splooosh*, and the Mojobot kept sinking, and then there was a *wooomf*.

Mojo had stopped moving.

He had hit bottom. He was at the bottom of Townsville Lake, which was under Townsville Bridge. Dirt and muck were all over the place...and water was starting to leak into the Mojobot!

If Mojo tries to fix the Mojobot, turn to page 17.

If Mojo decides to bail out and abandon the Mojobot, turn to page 46.

41

The Mayor's office it is, Mojo decided. He zoomed over there, figuring that he was ready for just about anything.

As he entered the Mayor's office, still inside his Mojobot, Mojo discovered that he couldn't be more wrong! Because standing there in the middle of the office was none other than that horrifyingly hair-styled villainess, Sedusa! She had the Mayor tucked neatly under one arm, with a blanket over his head! Clearly she was about to kidnap him!

"Well, well," purred Sedusa. "I wasn't expecting to see *you* here."

"Whoever you are," the Mayor cried out, his little legs pumping in the air, "I'll give you a huge reward if only you'll rescue me from Sedusa's clutches!"

"Ignore him," Sedusa told Mojo. "If you're smart—and I know you are—you'll want in on my fiendish plan."

Nervously, Mojo checked his power level indicators and found that he had reason for concern: His Punkium levels were starting to drop. The longer Mojo stood around here, the more chance there was that he'd be out of power by the time he'd really need it: Namely, when it was time to face The Powerpuff Girls.

If Mojo decides to join Sedusa in her plan, turn to page 48.

If Mojo decides to take on Sedusa to get the Mayor's reward offer, turn to page 24.

If Mojo decides to head out and keep trying to find The Powerpuff Girls, turn to page 18.

Since when is anyone expecting me, Mojo Jojo, to be the protector of Townsville? thought Mojo. *Since never, that's when! I don't need to worry about the tentacled menace because I have bigger fish...or squids...to fry.*

Mojo flew away from the scene in his Mojobot, but he suddenly heard shouting...and power-punching...and cheers....

"The Powerpuff Girls! Curse those Girls and their blasted timing!" groaned Mojo to himself. "They showed up the instant my back was turned!"

Immediately, Mojo headed back to the site of the squid's reign of terror...except it was all over! The monster was slinking away into the water, looking pretty thoroughly pummeled. The Girls had shown up, defeated the monster, and then taken off!

But where did they go? Mojo employed his high-powered vision device, and he saw what appeared to be a blond little girl—Bubbles, he hoped—flying in one direction, and a red-haired little girl—was it Blossom?—flying in the opposite direction! As good as the Mojobot might be, even *it* couldn't go in two directions at once!

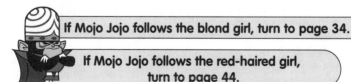

If Mojo Jojo follows the blond girl, turn to page 34.

If Mojo Jojo follows the red-haired girl, turn to page 44.

Mojo followed what he hoped was Blossom, only to be disappointed when he caught up with her. A red-haired girl *was* flying through the air, but she had frizzy, not straight, hair and was clearly *not* a nice person. "That's not Blossom at all!" snapped Mojo. "It's just Princess in a flying suit! It's that spoiled little rich girl who wants to be a Powerpuff Girl and is now one of their most constant and annoying opponents! Even more annoying than me! Not more evil...just more annoying."

But just as Mojo started to turn away, he noticed that Princess was carrying something under her arm. It appeared to be a rather impressive-looking jewel. Mojo didn't know where she had gotten it from, but he knew where he wanted it to go: straight into his

own personal collection of treasures!

Except he wasn't sure if he really had the time, or the energy reserves, to start tussling with Princess over a jewel, no matter how big and sparkling it might be.

If Mojo decides to try and get the jewel from Princess, turn to page 28.

If Mojo decides Princess is not worth his time and The Powerpuff Girls take first priority, turn to page 50.

"I'm just standing here?" asked Mojo. "Wait... why am I just standing here?! I cannot just stand here! I am a supervillain! A supervillain is decisive, determined, confident! A supervillain is swift, to the point, does not falter, waver, or change his mind, and makes prompt and immediate decisions without hesitation! Instead I'm just standing here like some sort of monkey statue! It's as if...as if some child, possibly sitting next to his or her parent, has given me a command, has chosen my path for me! Well, I am Mojo Jojo! I do not take commands! I give commands, and others obey! So just forget it! I'm not going to just stand here and do nothing!"

Turn back to page 53 and choose one of the other paths! Mojo has spoken!

45

Mojo realized that staying inside the Mojobot wasn't going to do him any good. As frustrating as it was for him to admit, he was going to have to abandon ship, as it were. He pushed against the escape hatch...but it wouldn't open! Long moments passed, and more and more water flooded in. Finally, Mojo was out of time. He had to try the hatch again—or he'd drown! This time, it opened. He pushed out into the water, swimming like crazy! The water was freezing. He felt like his lungs were going to explode as he swam as hard as he could.

And then...Mojo broke the surface! He gulped in huge breaths of air as he paddled over to the shore and pulled himself up. He looked around, but didn't see anyone. If The Powerpuff Girls were nearby, then they were doubtlessly underwater looking for him...and Mojo certainly didn't need to sit around here and wait for them to show up so they could drag him away to jail.

Continue on page 22.

Heck, Mojo always was a sucker for a really good evil plan.

Sedusa's plan, however, was amazingly simple. "We're going to kidnap the Mayor," she said, "and hold him for ransom. We'll clean out the entirety of the Townsville Treasury."

"Great idea!" Mojo said gleefully, using the telescope inside the Mojobot to focus on this month's treasury statement on the Mayor's desk, which said just how much money Townsville currently had. Mojo saw the number and his face fell. He looked in annoyance at Sedusa. "You are aware, are you not, that Townsville currently has only twenty-nine cents to its name?"

Sedusa looked less than thrilled at this news. From under the blanket, the Mayor said, "It was a slow month."

"Blast!" Mojo said, thumping hard on a file cabinet with a giant robotic fist. "You and your stupid plans, Sedusa!"

And suddenly one of the drawers in the cabinet flew open, and inside it was Blossom of The Powerpuff Girls, rubbing her eyes and looking around, confused! "Has anyone seen Buttercup? She's It and I guess I fell asleep waiting for her...," she said, and then she looked around in astonishment. "Mojo Jojo! Sedusa!"

"Oh! Blossom! I forgot you were hiding in here!" said the Mayor, recognizing her voice from under the blanket. "How's the hide-and-seek going?"

"Better than your day seems to be, Mr. Mayor! But don't worry...it's about to improve!" said Blossom.

Sedusa was about to attack Blossom, but Mojo used the Mojobot to push Sedusa aside. No one was going to have a shot at Blossom but Mojo!

Continue on page 14.

49

Deciding that Princess wasn't worth the trouble, no matter how tempting the jewel was, Mojo started to head off in another direction...and saw The Powerpuff Girls!

They hadn't spotted him yet, so he took refuge behind a nearby cloud. Peeking around the edges of the cloud, Mojo watched from a safe distance as the Girls rounded up Princess. *That foolish child is no match for The Powerpuff Girls!* Mojo thought. Cranking up his eavesdropping microphones, Mojo listened in on their conversation.

"Good thing we were between rounds of hide-and-seek when the alarm went off at the jewelry museum!" said Bubbles.

"It's mine! Give it back!" shouted Princess. "I absolutely need it! It'll go perfectly with the tiara I stole last week....Oh, nuts!" she said as she realized she'd just admitted to a crime she hadn't even been caught at.

The Powerpuff Girls laughed at Princess's frustration. "Okay, Bubbles, it's your turn to count, because you were it!" said Blossom. "I'll take Princess to the Townsville Jail, and Buttercup, you return the jewel to the museum! Then we'll go hide again."

"Okay," said Bubbles.

"Lemme go!" shouted Princess. "Somebody get me out of this! My daddy will pay a gazillion dollars!"

"Aw, stop your whining, there's nobody around to hear you," said Buttercup, unaware that Mojo was nearby. It made him want to laugh in villainous glee, but if he did that, they'd hear him with their supersonic hearing, so he clammed up.

"Be careful with that jewel, Buttercup," said Blossom. "It's got a core of pure Punkium, a very powerful and rare energy source. You wouldn't want it to fall into the wrong hands."

The Girls split off, and Mojo realized: Punkium! It could be enough to power his Mojobot for who knew how long! Time was ticking away. He could go after Buttercup, the source of his precious Punkium. But Bubbles, who was just floating there with her eyes shut, counting, was easy pickings...while Princess represented a gazillion dollars....

If Mojo takes on Buttercup so he can have a shot at grabbing the jewel, turn to page 58.

If Mojo goes after Bubbles, turn to page 34.

If Mojo takes on Blossom so that he can get a reward from Princess's grateful father, turn to page 10.

As Mojo arrived at the bank, he saw that it was being robbed—by the Gangreen Gang! Mojo looked around but there was still no sign of The Powerpuff Girls.

The problem was that once Mojo had succeeded in destroying The Powerpuff Girls and making Townsville safe for all sorts of evildoing, he had planned to follow up by cleaning out the bank himself!

"But how am I going to do that if the Gangreen Gang has already done it?" Mojo muttered to himself. "I could stop them, of course. They're no match for my mighty Mojobot. On the other hand, they are villains just like me...Mojo Jojo. Granted, they're not super-geniuses, and they're not covered with fur,

and they're not monkeys with giant brains, but otherwise, they're just like me! Should I really be attacking them? Not only does it seem not right, but it even seems...wrong."

Of course, Mojo could just stand around and see what, if anything, developed.

If Mojo decides to walk off and let the Gangreen Gang do what they want, turn to page 56.

If Mojo decides to simply stand there and wait to see what happens, turn to page 45.

If Mojo decides to stop the Gangreen Gang from robbing the bank so that he can take the money himself, turn to page 12.

And then, to Mojo's horror, the Girls said, "Good going, Mojo." Blossom was telling him, "We've been hearing about how you've been helping people and battling villains while we were off having fun! Great to have you aboard, fighting on behalf of the good guys!"

Mojo wanted to scream at them, to say, "You foolish Girls! I am evil! Evil, I tell you!" But if he did that, they'd just attack him, and he didn't have enough power left to take them on right then!

So all Mojo could do was grit his teeth and say, "Thank you, Girls," and slink away in total humiliation.

Continue on page 64.

Suddenly, there was a huge whooshing of water, and from the depths of Townsville Lake emerged the single biggest monster Mojo had ever seen. He was absolutely gigantic...and obviously he had noticed Mojo, because the monster looked at him, and then at Buttercup.

Then the monster spoke in a very polite, almost apologetic, voice as he said, "This is going to be a problem. I was going to fight *all* The Powerpuff Girls...I was really looking forward to defeating them this time...but you've gone and defeated one already. I'm afraid that makes me very, very angry... and I'm going to have to take that out on you."

Big as the monster was, Mojo was sure that it would be no match for his Mojobot. And if Mojo waited by the bridge, the other two Girls would be sure to show up to fight the monster, and then he could defeat them, too! At least Mojo *hoped* he could—it looked like Buttercup was recovering quickly....

Continue on page 40.

Mojo decided that it was more important to honor the villainous brotherhood he shared with the other evildoers of Townsville...and so off he went, leaving the Gangreen Gang to do their dirty work.

Arcing through the air, Mojo studied all of his instruments, trying to locate where those cursed and annoying Girls might be. His radar swept the sky, all his detection devices turned up to the max....

"Aha! I have found something...well, two things, actually!" Mojo said to himself. "About a mile away, there seems to be a red-haired little girl hurtling through the air at a distance. It's probably that disgustingly nice Blossom.

"And in the other direction, there's a gargantuan monster stomping across the Townsville Bridge, which stands over the proud Townsville Lake." Mojo saw that the creature was causing disaster wherever it stomped, and would most likely draw Blossom and her sisters, Buttercup and Bubbles, over to the bridge as soon as they found out about it. Then he'd have the chance to test his wonderful Mojobot against all three Girls at once! But if Mojo went to the bridge, he'd have to be pretty careful that the monster didn't decide to go after *him* instead!

If Mojo decides to check out the little red-haired girl to see who it is, turn to page 44.

If Mojo decides to go after the monster, turn to page 40.

Mojo couldn't pass up that potential supply of Punkium. He barreled after Buttercup, who had the jewel safely tucked under her arm. She was directly ahead of him now, and since she didn't know Mojo was following her, naturally she didn't realize just how close behind her he was.

"Target acquired," Mojo muttered as he aimed his laser, "and...fire!"

Mojo uncorked both barrels of his laser, and the powerful weapon slammed into Buttercup before she even realized Mojo was there! Buttercup flipped end over end and dropped the jewel! Mojo caught it with no problem. It was his!

"You give that back, Mojo!" shouted Buttercup, but she was already woozy from the previous blast, and he was not about to let up on her. Another laser blast from the Mojobot was enough to send Buttercup into a tailspin! Mojo followed her down, down, as she spiraled toward the Townsville Bridge and landed on the ground. Mojo had done it! He had defeated one of The Powerpuff Girls!

Mojo shoved the jewel into the power supply of the Mojobot and grinned fiendishly as the power levels jumped back to the top! The Mojobot was fully recharged! Nothing could hurt him now...except for, maybe, a monster. And maybe the other two Powerpuff Girls. But other than that, he was in the clear!

Continue on page 55.

As Mojo sat there in his sinking Mojobot, keeping his searchlight turned off, Buttercup shot off, leaving a wake of water behind her. In the meantime, the Mojobot was now filled almost entirely with water. Mojo had managed to preserve his precious pride...but at what cost? He tried shoving at the escape hatch, but it appeared to be jammed. *This is* not *one of my better days*, Mojo thought in despair.

Continue on page 63.

*And so, once again, the day is saved...by
The Powerpuff Girls! Better luck next time, Mojo!*

Yes, Mojo was feeling pretty darned proud of himself.

That is, until Blossom and Buttercup showed up, looking mad as anything over what he'd done to their sister, and preparing to attack! And Mojo had drained his Punkium supply in his earlier fight! He was no longer invincible, and because of that, it looked like Townsville Jail was about to become his new home! Again.

Continue on page 61.

But suddenly, a monstrous hand picked up Mojo, wrapping around the Mojobot and sealing off any more water from flooding in.

It was Steve, the monster. With his voice burbling through the water, Steve said, "Maybe The Powerpuff Girls defeated me, but at least I'll have a nice souvenir to bring back to Monster Isle." He popped the Mojobot into his mouth for safekeeping. In the distance, Mojo heard a faint sound. It was the noise made by three superpowered little Girls flying quickly through the air. The good news for Mojo was that it seemed as if The Powerpuff Girls were going to rescue him from becoming a souvenir on a shelf in a monster's house back on Monster Isle. The bad news was, he was being saved by The Powerpuff Girls!

"How embarrassing!" Mojo groaned.

Continue on page 61.

And so the day is saved by...Mojo Jojo?!?!?

THE END